America's Leaders

The First Lady
of the United States

by Joanne Mattern

BLACKBIRCH® PRESS

San Diego • Detroit • New York • San Francisco • Cleveland • New Haven, Conn. • Waterville, Maine • London • Munich

© 2003 by Blackbirch Press™. Blackbirch Press™ is an imprint of The Gale Group, Inc., a division of Thomson Learning, Inc.

Blackbirch Press™ and Thomson Learning™ are trademarks used herein under license.

For more information, contact
The Gale Group, Inc.
27500 Drake Rd.
Farmington Hills, MI 48331-3535
Or you can visit our Internet site at http://www.gale.com

ALL RIGHTS RESERVED
No part of this work covered by the copyright hereon may be reproduced or used in any form or by any means—graphic, electronic, or mechanical, including photocopying, recording, taping, Web distribution or information storage retrieval systems—without the written permission of the publisher.

Every effort has been made to trace the owners of copyrighted material.

Photo credits: Cover, back cover © Creatas; Martha Washington cover inset, pages 6, 8, 26, 27, 28 © Library of Congress; Lady Bird Johnson cover inset © LBJ Library Collection; Laura Bush cover inset © The White House; The White House cover inset © Corel Corporation; pages 4, 5, 29, 31 © Blackbirch Press Archives; pages 7, 9, 12, 13, 14, 15, 17, 19, 20, 22, 23, 25, 27 © CORBIS; pages 9, 10, 18 © Dover Publications; page 11 © National Archives; page 16 © FDR Library Public Domain; page 21 © National Portrait Gallery

LIBRARY OF CONGRESS CATALOGING-IN-PUBLICATION DATA

Mattern, Joanne, 1963–
 The First Lady / by Joanne Mattern.
    p. cm. — (America's leaders series)
 Summary: Discusses the role of the wife of the president of the United States, known as the first lady, and shows a schedule for what might be considered a typical day.
 Includes bibliographical references and index.
 ISBN 1-56711-264-1 (alk. paper)
 1. Presidents' spouses—United States—Juvenile literature. 2. Presidents' spouses—United States—History—Juvenile literature. 3. Presidents' spouses—United States—Biography—Juvenile literature. [1. First lady.] I. Title. II. Series.
E176.2.M27 2003
352.23—dc21
                                                                    2002011727

Printed in United States
10 9 8 7 6 5 4 3 2 1

Table of Contents

An Unofficial Position 4

A Changing Role 8

On the Job 14

Where Does the First Lady Work? 16

Who Works with the First Lady? 17

A Special Challenge .18

A Time of Crisis 20

Another Time of Crisis 22

A First Lady's Day 24

Fascinating Facts 26

Glossary 29

For More Information 30

Index 32

An Unofficial Position

More than 200 years ago, a group of men wrote a document, the U.S. Constitution, which established the American government. The authors of the Constitution split the government into three branches—the legislative branch, the judicial branch, and the executive branch.

Under the Constitution, the legislative branch was made up of the Senate and the House of Representatives. The judicial branch was the nation's court system, with the Supreme Court as the highest court. The third branch of government, the executive branch, was led by the president.

The president has a staff of people who advise him and help him make decisions. One of his most important advisers, however, does not hold an official

The U.S. Constitution established the American government.

President Jimmy Carter and his wife, Rosalynn. The first lady has an important, though unofficial, position.

position. This adviser is the president's wife. She is called the first lady.

The first lady is not elected or appointed. She gets her position simply because she is married to the president. Despite her unofficial position, the first lady can be one of the most powerful and interesting figures in the government.

> **USA Fact**
> Although the first lady puts in long hours and handles many kinds of duties, she is not paid for her work.

Women known as suffragists worked for laws that gave women the right to vote.

Even though many of them were intelligent and well educated, the early first ladies usually stayed behind the scenes. This was mainly because they lived at a time when women did not have much political power. Until the 20th century, most people felt that a woman's job was to take care of her home and raise children. Women could not even vote until 1920. As a result, early first ladies never made speeches or campaigned on their own. Most kept their opinions to themselves, because everyone expected them to have the same views as their husbands.

Until recent years, reporters and the public were more interested in what the first lady wore or how she decorated the White House than in what she thought or said. In the late 20th century, women gained more rights and respect. This helped first ladies win more responsibilities and influence. Today, people expect first ladies to have their own opinions and take actions that make a difference in the world.

First Lady Rosalynn Carter (third from left) attends a political rally.

A Changing Role

Most early first ladies had little power. Their main duty was to serve as hostess when the president had important guests or held state dinners. Dolley Madison, wife of President James Madison, was one of the most famous hostesses in the United States. She loved to give parties. During her years as first lady, the White House was the social center of Washington, D.C. Every Wednesday night, she held parties called "drawing rooms." Many different people came to these parties. Among the guests were artists, politicians, businessmen, and writers.

Dolley Madison loved to have parties at the White House.

Abigail Adams, wife of second president John Adams, was unique among early first ladies. Unlike other women of her day, she expected her husband to treat her as an equal. Adams followed politics and world affairs closely.

First Ladies
Political Role ❖ Public Image

The Smithsonian Institution's National Museum of American History in Washington, D.C., has a special section that displays the dresses and other accessories of the nation's first ladies.

She shared her strong views with the president. John Adams greatly respected his wife and took her advice seriously. Newspapers and the public, on the other hand, were often critical of her outspokenness.

Unlike most early first ladies, Abigail Adams was deeply interested in politics and current events.

Margaret Taylor was rarely seen in public.

Most first ladies stayed out of the public eye. Margaret Taylor, the wife of President Zachary Taylor, for instance, spent most of her time in the private rooms of the White House. Most Americans did not even know what she looked like.

In the 1930s, Eleanor Roosevelt transformed the role of first lady during the four terms of her husband, President Franklin D. Roosevelt. Franklin Roosevelt had been disabled by polio in 1921, when he was 39 years old. He had to use a wheelchair or braces and crutches to get around. This made it difficult for him to travel around the country and talk with Americans. His wife came to the rescue. She visited people all over the United States and saw how they lived. Then she went home and told her husband what she had seen and heard. Thanks to his wife's work, the president learned about the problems and challenges that the American people faced.

Eleanor Roosevelt was not shy when she wanted to express her opinions. She gave speeches all over the world. For many years, she wrote a daily newspaper column called "My Day." She worked hard to help victims of poverty, war, and racial prejudice. After her husband died in 1945, she remained a well-known public figure until her own death in 1962.

USA Fact

After World War II ended in 1945, an organization was set up to try to stop future wars. It was called the United Nations (UN). Eleanor Roosevelt was a member of the group that attended the first UN meetings in December 1945. She also led the Commission on Human Rights and helped write the UN Declaration of Human Rights.

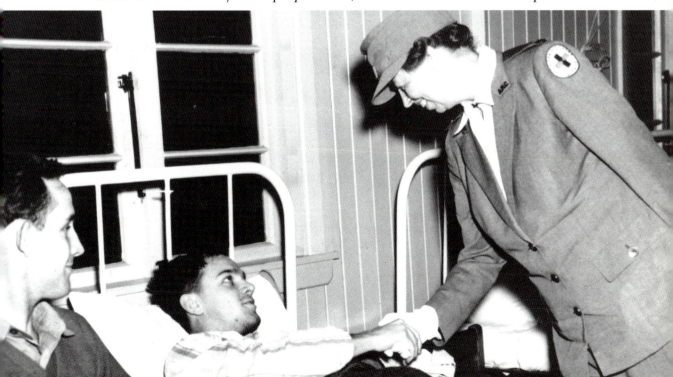

Eleanor Roosevelt (right) traveled all over the world and told her husband about the concerns of other people. Here, she visits a soldier in a hospital.

Nancy Reagan started the antidrug "Just Say No" campaign in 1985.

USA Fact

The "Just Say No" program to end drug abuse began in 1985 at a grammar school in Oakland, California. It told children to simply "Just Say No" when someone offered them drugs or alcohol. The antidrug message spread across the nation, thanks to the efforts of First Lady Nancy Reagan.

First ladies who came after Eleanor Roosevelt followed her example, and used their position to make people aware of social issues.

Lady Bird Johnson, wife of President Lyndon Johnson, worked to make the United States more beautiful. Her idea was to get rid of billboards and add gardens to public spaces. President Ronald Reagan's wife, Nancy, fought drug abuse with her "Just Say No" campaign, aimed at young Americans. Barbara Bush, wife of President George Bush, traveled around the United States to push for programs to help both children and adults learn to read.

As first lady, Barbara Bush promoted reading programs.

On the Job

Today, the first lady takes part in many activities. The days are long gone when she could focus only on her home and her family, and act as if she did not have an opinion. The American people expect first ladies to be involved in social causes and to lead an active public life. Most first ladies have welcomed the opportunity to make their mark on society. They want to gain support for causes that are important to them.

In 1979, Rosalynn Carter testified before Congress about health issues.

The first lady often attends meetings in the White House that deal with social issues she has taken an interest in. She may also attend congressional hearings and other governmental activities that deal with important issues.

The first lady also spends much of her time traveling. Sometimes, she goes abroad with the president to visit foreign leaders and other world figures. They usually fly on the presidential plane, *Air Force One*, to places around the world.

First Lady Laura Bush spoke with Afghan president Hamid Karzai before George W. Bush's 2002 State of the Union speech. First ladies often meet world leaders.

At other times, the first lady travels alone. She may go to schools or community centers to give speeches on issues that concern her or the president. She also might represent the United States at important world events, such as the funeral or wedding of a world leader.

Like the first ladies who lived long ago, today's first lady serves as a hostess at state dinners and parties. These events are held at the White House to honor and entertain important guests. Guests may include world leaders, political or economic advisers, and respected figures in arts and entertainment. White House dinners feature elaborate meals made by chefs. After dinner, there is usually music and dancing. The first lady's role is to meet and talk with each of the guests, make everyone feel at ease, and help them have a good time.

Where Does the First Lady Work?

The first lady traditionally has had an office in the East Wing of the White House. When Hillary Clinton, wife of President Bill Clinton, was first lady, however, she moved her office to the West Wing of the White House. There she could be closer to the president's advisers.

In addition to her office, the first lady lives with the president and their family at the White House. The first family has private quarters upstairs in the White House, where they can live away from the public eye.

Eleanor Roosevelt (right) had her office in the East Wing of the White House.

Who Works with the First Lady?

Like the president, the first lady has her own staff. Advisers make sure she has the most up-to-date information about world affairs, social concerns, and other news. The first lady also has several secretaries. Some of them answer mail and phone calls, write statements for the press, or make travel arrangements.

Other secretaries make appointments and set up a daily schedule for the first lady. This helps her find time for all her duties. Many groups ask the first lady to speak at special ceremonies, such as a graduation or the opening of a community center. The first lady also represents her husband at events in the United States and abroad. Her day must be carefully planned to make sure she can take care of everything she has to do.

Like other first ladies, Hillary Rodham Clinton had her own staff of advisers and secretaries.

A Special Challenge

The role of first lady presents a unique challenge. First ladies do not run for office, but they are public figures nonetheless. Many first ladies have been uncomfortable with the attention they receive from the press and the public. People want to know everything they say, do, or wear. Martha Washington, the first woman to be first lady, found the lack of privacy hard to bear. "I am more like a state prisoner than anything else," she said.

For security reasons, first ladies cannot go out in public without Secret Service officers to protect them at all times. This can be inconvenient both for the first lady and for others. Once, when Barbara Bush wanted to take a walk in a Washington, D.C., park, the Secret Service closed the park to the public so she could stroll safely.

Martha Washington was uncomfortable with the attention she received as first lady.

USA Fact

Betty Ford was the only first lady whose husband was never elected. Gerald Ford was appointed to be President Richard Nixon's vice president in 1973, after Vice President Spiro Agnew resigned. Ford then became president in 1974, when Nixon resigned the presidency in the midst of a scandal.

Sometimes, first ladies have used their loss of privacy to help other people. While she was first lady, Betty Ford, wife of Gerald Ford, was diagnosed with breast cancer. She spoke out about the disease and her treatment. Thanks to her example, thousands of women were tested for cancer. Ford said the experience helped her "recognize more clearly the power of the woman in the White House. Not my power, but the power of the position, a power which could be used to help."

Betty Ford used her position as first lady to teach women about breast cancer.

A Time of Crisis

Most of the time, the first lady's job is fairly uneventful. Several first ladies, however, have faced danger and tragedy on the job. During these times of crisis, the nation looked to the first lady as a model of courage and leadership.

Dolley Madison rescued important documents and a portrait of George Washington during the War of 1812.

One of the most dramatic events in American history happened when Dolley Madison was first lady during the War of 1812. In late August 1814, the British army attacked Washington, D.C. President James Madison had already left the White House to meet with one of his

USA Fact

Mary Todd Lincoln, wife of Abraham Lincoln, was first lady during the Civil War (1861–1865). She had been born in the Southern state of Kentucky, but she supported the Union in the war. As a result, Southerners called her a traitor, while people loyal to the Union believed she worked to help the South during the war.

generals. His wife and her staff were planning to meet them later. As British troops came closer, the first lady gathered important papers. She ordered her staff to load a wagon with paintings and other valuables so they would not fall into the hands of the British. One of the items she rescued was a portrait of George Washington. The first lady refused to leave until the picture was removed. Dolley Madison and her staff managed to escape just ahead of the British army. Because of her bravery and quick thinking, the painting—an important national treasure—was saved for future generations to enjoy.

This portrait of George Washington was removed from the White House before British troops arrived in 1814.

Another Time of Crisis

First Lady Jacqueline Kennedy faced a challenge of a different kind. On November 22, 1963, she went with her husband, President John F. Kennedy, on a campaign trip to Texas. That afternoon, the president and the first lady were riding in an open car through the streets of Dallas. Suddenly, shots rang out. A man named Lee Harvey Oswald had fired a rifle from an upper floor of a nearby building, the Texas School Book Depository.

Jacqueline Kennedy watched as Lyndon B. Johnson was sworn in as president in 1963.

Jacqueline Kennedy attended her husband's funeral in 1963.

President Kennedy was shot in the head. He was rushed to the hospital, where he soon died. Americans were shocked and saddened by the loss of their young, popular president. Mrs. Kennedy became the role model for the nation in its sorrow. She stood by bravely as the new president, Lyndon Johnson, was sworn in. She also remained calm and controlled during her husband's funeral, and set a courageous example for her two young children, Caroline and John Jr. Americans and other people around the world admired her strength in the face of terrible grief.

A First Lady's Day

The first lady's day is packed with activities, both public and private. Here is what a schedule might be like for the first lady.

6:00 AM	Wakes, showers, dresses, watches television news
7:00 AM	Has breakfast with the president
8:00 AM	Meets with secretaries to go over the day's schedule
9:15 AM	Boards plane to travel to make a speech
11:00 AM	Arrives at her speaking engagement and is met by representatives of the charity to which she will speak
11:30 AM	Speaks to the charity group and attends a luncheon
1:30 PM	Boards plane to return to Washington, D.C.
3:00 PM	Meets with a reporter for a magazine interview
4:00 PM	Meets with congressional representatives about social issues
5:30 PM	Returns to White House to dress for dinner

President George W. Bush and First Lady Laura Bush board Air Force One. The first lady does a lot of traveling.

7:00 PM	Has dinner with the president and members of the business community
10:30 PM	Returns to the family quarters and prepares for bed
11:30 PM	Bed

Fascinating Facts

Mary Todd Lincoln deeply mourned the death of her son, Willie. She held rituals in the White House to try to get in touch with his spirit, and believed she saw his ghost at night.

Many early first ladies did not attend their husbands' inaugurations. **Helen Taft**, wife of William Howard Taft, was the first president's wife to ride beside her husband on Inauguration Day.

At William Taft's inauguration, Helen Taft became the first wife of a president to ride with her husband to the White House after the inauguration ceremony.

James Buchanan was the only U.S. president who was not married. His niece, **Harriet Lane**, filled the role of first lady for him. Martin Van Buren was a widower when he was elected president. His daughter-in-law served as his hostess at social events. Other presidents also had other family members perform the first lady's duties because their wives were ill or not up to the job.

Harriet Lane

Lucy Hayes, wife of Rutherford B. Hayes, was called "Lemonade Lucy" because she refused to serve alcohol at the White House.

Hillary Clinton is the only first lady to hold an elected office of her own. After her husband left the White House in 2001, she was elected as a U.S. senator from New York.

Hillary Clinton

Frances Cleveland

Frances Cleveland was only 21 years old when she married Grover Cleveland at the White House. She was the youngest first lady.

Edith Wilson may have made important national decisions while her husband, Woodrow Wilson, was disabled by a stroke. For several weeks, she screened every question and issue that was brought to the president's attention. Some historians believe that she made decisions for him, and signed his name on bills and legal documents. She denied this, and said, "I never made a single decision regarding public affairs myself—the only decision that was mine was what was important and what was not."

Mamie Eisenhower (right) visited Bess Truman at the White House in 1952.

Glossary

adviser—someone who works closely with a person in power and provides information and suggestions

Air Force One—a jet built especially for the president and his family

brief—to give someone information so that person can do his or her job

campaign—a series of actions, such as speeches and public appearances, done to win votes for an election

Congress—the legislative branch of government, composed of the Senate and the House of Representatives

Constitution—the document that established the United States and set forth the principles of the nation

inauguration—the process by which an elected official is admitted to office

Secret Service—a group of officers whose job is to protect the president and his family

Bess Truman served as first lady from 1945 to 1953.

For More Information

Publications

Clinton, Susan Maloney. *First Ladies*. Chicago: Childrens Press, 1994.

Feinberg, Barbara Silberdick. *America's First Ladies: Changing Expectations*. New York: Franklin Watts, 1998.

Mayo, Edith P., ed. *The Smithsonian Book of the First Ladies*. New York: Henry Holt, 1996.

Websites

First Ladies Around the World

www.womenshistory.about.com/cs/firstladies

Includes links to articles and Web sites about all U.S. first ladies.

Information on First Ladies and Their Roles at the Inaugurations

www.zweb.com/parpro/inauguration.html

An entertaining list of facts on the role of first ladies at every inauguration from George Washington's to George W. Bush's.

Inside the East Wing

www.whitehouse.gov/firstlady

This official White House site includes news about and speeches given by the current first lady, as well as biographies of previous first ladies.

National First Ladies' Library

www.firstladies.org

This is the Web page of the National First Ladies' Library, located in Ida McKinley's house in Canton, Ohio. The site includes information about the library's collections, and a bibliography of important documents related to first ladies.

President Richard Nixon and his wife, Pat, visited China in 1972.

Index

Adams, Abigail 8–10
Advisers 4, 16, 17
Air Force One 14, 25
Bush, Barbara 13, 18
Bush, Laura 25
Bush, George W. 25
Carter, Rosalynn 5, 7, 14
Cleveland, Frances 27
Clinton, Hillary 16, 28
Congressional hearings 14
Constitution, the 4
"Drawing rooms" 8
East Wing 16
Ford, Betty 18, 19
Government branches 4
Hayes, Lucy 28
Hostess 8, 15, 27
Inauguration 26
Johnson, Lady Bird 13
Johnson, Lyndon B. 13, 23
"Just Say No" 12, 13
Kennedy, Jacqueline 22–23
Kennedy, John F. 22-23
Lane, Harriet 27
Lincoln, Mary Todd 20, 26
Madison, Dolley 8, 20–21
Madison, James 8, 20
"My Day" 12
Oswald, Lee Harvey 22
Polio 10
Reagan, Nancy 12, 13
Roosevelt, Eleanor 10–13
Roosevelt, Franklin, D. .10–11, 12
Secretaries 17, 24
Secret Service 18
Speeches 6, 12, 15, 17, 24
Taft, Helen 26
Taft, William Howard 26
Taylor, Margaret 10
Taylor, Zachary 10
United Nations 11
War of 1812 20–21
Washington, George 21
Washington, Martha 18
West Wing 16
Wilson, Edith 27
Women's right to vote 6